Pascal Biet

A Cultivated Wolf

Story by Becky Bloom

SIPHANO PICTURE BOOKS

After many days' walking, the Wolf wandered into a quiet little town. He was tired and hungry and his feet were aching, and he had only a little money that he kept for emergencies.

Then he remembered. There's a farm outside this village, he thought. I'll find some food there....

As he peered over the farm fence he saw a pig, a duck and a cow reading in the sun.

The Wolf had never seen animals read before. My eyes are playing tricks on me, thought the Wolf. But he was hungry and didn't think about it too much.

The Wolf stood up tall, took a deep breath...

...and pounced at the animals with a howl:

«Aaa-OOOOO-ooo!»

Chickens and rabbits ran for their lives, but the Duck,
the Pig and the Cow didn't budge.

«What is that awful noise?» complained the Cow «I can't
concentrate on my book.»

«Just ignore it,» said the Duck.

The Wolf did not like to be ignored.

«What's wrong with you?» asked the Wolf. «Can't you see I'm a big and dangerous wolf?»

«I'm sure you are,» replied the Pig. «But couldn't you be big and dangerous somewhere else? We're trying to read. This is a farm for cultivated animals. Now be a good wolf and go away,» said the Pig, and gave him a push.

The Wolf had never been treated like this before.

«Cultivated animals.... Cultivated animals!» the Wolf repeated to himself. «This is something new. Well, then! I will learn how to read, too!» And off he went to school.

The children found it strange to have a wolf in their class, but, as he didn't try to eat anyone, they soon got used to him. The Wolf was serious and hardworking, and after much effort he learned to read and write. Soon he became the best in the class.

Feeling quite satisfied, the Wolf went back to the farm and jumped over the fence. I'll show them, he thought.

He opened his book and began to read:

Run, wolf! run!
See wolf run.

«You've got a long way to go,» said the Duck, without even bothering to look up. And the Pig, the Duck, and the Cow went on reading their own books, not in the least impressed.

The Wolf jumped back over the fence and ran...

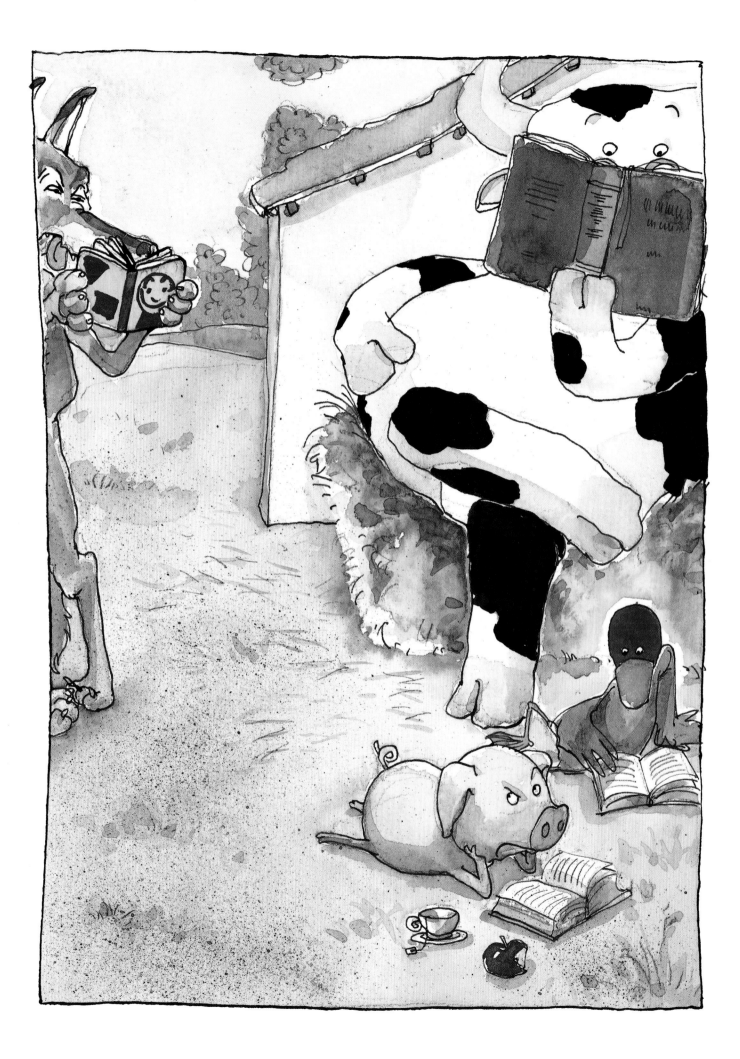

...straight to the public library. He studied long and hard, reading lots of dusty old books, and he practised and practised until he could read without stopping.

«I must be good enough for them now,» he said to himself.

The Wolf walked up to the farm gate and knocked. This will surely impress them, he thought.

The Wolf opened *The Three Little Pigs* and began to read:

OnceuponatimethereweretthreelittlepigsOnedaytheirmother calledthemandtoldthem...

«Stop this racket,» interrupted the Duck.

«You have improved,» remarked the Pig, «but you still need to work on your style.»

The Wolf tucked his tail between his legs and slunk away.

But the Wolf wasn't going to give up. He counted the little money he had left and he went to the bookshop and bought a splendid new storybook. His first Very Own Book!

He was going to read it day and night, every letter and every line. He would read so well that the farm animals would admire him.

«Ding-dong,» rang the Wolf at the farm gate.

He lay down on the grass, made himself comfortable, took out his new book and began to read.

He read with confidence and passion, and the Pig, the Cow and the Duck all listened and said not one word.

Each time he finished a story, the Pig, the Cow and the Duck asked the Wolf if he would please read them another.

So the Wolf read on, story after story. One minute he was a genie emerging from a lamp, the next Little Red Riding-hood, and then a swashbuckling pirate.

«This is so much fun,» said the Duck.
«He's a master,» said the Pig.
«Why don't you join us on our picnic today?» offered the Cow.

And so they all had a picnic, the Pig, the Cow, the Duck and the Wolf. They lay in the long grass and told stories all the afternoon long.

«We should all become storytellers,» said the Cow suddenly.
«We could travel around the world,» added the Duck.
«We can start tomorrow morning,» said the Pig.
The Wolf stretched in the grass. He was happy to have such wonderful friends.